A Deep Space Disappearance

Evans took a deep breath. "Senior Tech McHugh is missing."

"What do you mean, missing? In case you've forgotten, this is a deep space vessel, Evans. No one can get in or out."

"I understand, ma'am. I made sure to investigate before I brought this to you. Just like you taught us."

"I also taught you about the geo-sensor, didn't I?" Sue tapped the tiny bump hidden in the hair above her right ear. "Mr. McHugh is an experienced member of our crew. He would not simply disappear, even if he *could*."

"Yes, ma'am, the tracking screen was the first thing I checked. Pull it up if you could, please, and we'll make sure."

Sue's eyes darted to the crew count, and her whole body flashed hot, then cold and clammy.

"Eight thousand seven hundred fifty-three," she whispered. "That can't be right. Even if he were dead…"

She switched over to the specific report on McHugh, and a deeper chill ran through her.

The yellow of Invalid flashed behind his name.

Not the normal green that every single other person showed, or the sad black of the deceased that Sue hadn't yet had to deal with on *Bellagos*.

Not one other person showed that impossible status.

To all of my fellow IT folks
Past, present, and recovering.

The world changes, but IT challenges remain the same.

THE CHANGES CASCADE

KARI KILGORE

SPIRAL PUBLISHING, LTD.

Chapter 1

Systems and Security Chief Sue Warrell watched the main security console, endless alerts and questions and worries running across the screen and through her mind. The command pod was small, only five paces across with dark gray curved walls and ceiling, but she loved the secure, comfortable feel of the space.

The chilly temperatures required for the thousands of comps that kept the ship running were a bonus to what she called her high metabolism.

Here more than anywhere else in the vast, interconnected series of living pods, production pods, and mechanical pods that made up *Expedition Mission Bellagos*, Sue felt at peace.

But today her normally calm and sedate console flashed orange and yellow rather than her beloved green. She was surprised and strangely irritated that not a single one of them advanced into the red of a confirmed failure.

The problem, the worst one in her long career in interstellar security, wasn't anything as dramatic as a debris strike, onboard systems failure, or a careless adjustment by one of the thousands of crewmembers.

Sue had been through more variations of those disasters than she cared to count, if she had the spare brainpower for counting. She was an expert at pinpointing, solving, and figuring out how to prevent bad choices and bad reactions, or she never would have beaten out thousands of other applicants for this multi-generational mission.

Nothing in her training or experience or her vivid imagination had prepared her for a nightmare straight out of the infancy of the digital age, one only Sue's youthful obsession with tech history gave her the means to recognize.

A corrupted systems upgrade from Earth HQ had infested the vessel's operations, interrupting one function after another before anyone realized what was happening. Since a neuro-alarm jarred her out of the hectic routine of getting ready for the supposedly routine update three days ago, Sue and nearly everyone else on board had been on emergency response status.

The nearly two-day-cycle message transit time between *Bellagos* and Earth HQ wasn't helping. Sue had sent the alert immediately, but she had no control over sheer distance and time. And she didn't know the massive software packages nearly as well as she knew the systems that depended on them

Rolling everything back without knowing more—and without assistance from HQ—could make bad enough trouble even worse.

She leaned back, the chair adjusting to her new posture with a faint sigh, and clenched her hands into fists to relieve the stress of hours of non-stop motion over the touch screens. Bio-engineers had perfected the nutrients and stimulants for sleepless days many years ago, ushering in a new age of technological advancement along with chronic overwork. The stims were safe enough if you didn't push past more than a week with no sleep, though Sue had never gotten used to the bitter, metallic taste and low ringing in her ears that went along with them.

She'd hacked the override on the audible alarms that made the ringing worse years ago, and she blessed that bit of rule breaking if no other.

Unfortunately all the hydro-showers in the galaxy wouldn't keep the oily stink of stress sweat from building up again. Not until she got some real sleep.

Stims aside, her body reacted to the strain of hours of tapping each orange alert into Investigate status, dispatching someone to the affected sector, and shifting the alert into the yellow of Invalid. Sometimes multiple times on the same blasted alert, and still no reds of confirmed trouble. Noting the fakes on her touch tablet slowed her down too much.

For the last several hours, she'd been relying on her brain's built-in ability to notice details and understand patterns.

Sue leaned forward, stretching her fingers against her thighs as the chair shifted her into a new angle. She was moving to tap eleven alerts into Invalid status when a piercing alarm broke through her silence hacks. The bass entrance request bong for the door behind her sounded at the same time. Her skull and all of her bones echoed the wretched noise.

"Blast these damn overrides!"

Sue pivoted to the right to slap the door status to Unlocked, then slid all ten fingers upward on the touchscreen to bring up the virtual keyboard. Before she could start typing, the door hissed open.

"What is it?" Sue said, not turning around. "I ordered Emergency Response Status hours ago, meaning no interruption. It better be good."

"Ma'am, I am so sorry to intrude," a low voice said.

Sue continued to type, growing more desperate to silence that screeching alarm by the millisecond.

Younger. Male. Odd musical accent, likely the southeastern sector of United North America.

Respectful, but brave enough to face her temper during a mess like this.

"What is it, Mr. Evans?"

The alarm stopped, and Sue let out a breath and shifted her knotted shoulders. She turned to face Security Tech Brandon Evans. He was tall enough to have to hunch a bit to keep more than his thick brown hair from brushing the ceiling, and he was wringing his hands. She'd never known Evans to be the nervous type.

That's when unease started gnawing around the stress in Sue's belly.

"We've had a problem, ma'am, one I can't leave to anyone else but you."

"It can't possibly be more of a problem than this." Sue waved an aching hand at the console as another eight lights shifted from green to orange.

"Well, I'm sorry, Chief, but it is." Evans took a deep breath. "Senior Tech McHugh is missing."

"What the hell do you mean, missing? In case you've forgotten, this is a deep space vessel, Evans. No one can get in or out."

The gnawing warmed up, much like the lumbar stress relief protocols of her chair kneading against her lower back.

"I understand, ma'am. I made sure to investigate before I brought this to you. Just like you taught us."

"I also taught you about the geo-sensor, didn't I?" Sue tapped the tiny bump hidden in the hair above her right ear even as the gnawing in her belly picked up speed. "Mr. McHugh is an experienced member of our crew. He would not simply disappear, even if he *could*."

"Yes, ma'am, the tracking screen was the first thing I checked after his son reported him missing. Pull it up if you could, please, and we'll make sure."

Sue pushed off with her foot, the numbness spreading through her body keeping her from using the right amount of force. The chair compensated and brought her in front of the ship status console. After three shaky tries, she brought up the tracking screen.

Her eyes darted to the crew count, and her whole body flashed hot, then cold and clammy.

"Eight thousand seven hundred fifty-three," she whispered. "That can't be right. Even if he were dead…"

She switched over to the specific report on McHugh, and a deeper chill ran through her.

The yellow of Invalid flashed behind his name.

Not the normal green that every single other person showed, or the sad black of the deceased that Sue hadn't yet had to deal with on *Bellagos*.

Not one other crewmember showed that impossible status.

"No one has seen him for more than twelve hours," Evans said, wringing his hands again. "I knew you'd want me to check with you first, Chief."

Sue stared at the screen, re-reading that impossible number. She didn't have to count to know one-third of the systems were now in Invalid, with another quarter still in Alert and under investigation.

She also didn't need any procedures training to realize she could not possibly deal with one more emergency.

The raging fire in her gut told her that, impossible or not, another had landed in her lap.

"I tried to replay his location for the last day cycle," Evans said. "Observation recordings, too. Neither system is online."

"Along with half the systems in this slow-motion disaster." A quick glance confirmed the whole recording suite was locked in Invalid mode. "Non-essential systems my ass. The data should still be there, but we can't get at it until I clear everything else."

"Are we any closer to bringing everything offline for a reset, ma'am?"

"Not until we hear back from Earth HQ and the Great Update Disaster stops knocking things offline at random. Can't take the chance of missing a real alarm or making everything worse trying to fix it."

Sue groaned, rubbing her face. "Okay, Evans, you did the right thing. You're taking lead on this since you obviously know how easily a panic can spread with everyone on edge. Let me see if I can get ahead of this. Bring his son in for a talk. Quietly."

Chapter 2

BY THE TIME Evans made it back an hour later, Sue and her overworked crew had wrangled all the remaining false alarms down to Invalid status. Nothing new had tripped over for half an hour. As long as she ignored the maddening clumps of yellow across all sectors of her console, she could tell herself things were under control.

A hearty swallow of a ginger-laced calming infusion she and everyone else involved in this update disaster carried constantly had settled her belly to a reasonable level of discomfort.

At least this time, Evans had the decency—or self-preservation instinct—to use a text alert to get her to open the door rather than the skull-splitting alarm.

Sue blinked, ignoring what felt like grit in her eyes, when she saw McHugh's son huddled behind the lanky Evans. The boy was years younger than she'd thought, probably not yet out of his first decade. His rumpled dark green pants and tunic showed no signs of rank or assignment, only his name on his chest just under his left shoulder. He had McHugh's wavy brown hair and bright blue eyes, but he was barely waist-high to Evans.

Eyes obviously red and swollen from crying, not from being awake for days like Sue's.

"This is Liam McHugh." Evans stepped to the side, but he didn't push the boy forward. "He reported his father missing."

Sue resisted a strong urge to bark orders at Evans, or maybe to get up and storm out herself.

Anything to avoid focusing on the kid's frightened and hopeful face.

"Thank you for letting us know, Liam." She leaned forward, deciding not to unfold herself from the chair just yet. Liam looked like he'd bolt at one sharp noise. After hours of sitting, she'd grunt loud enough to scare him *and* Evans. "You were born on board *Bellagos*?"

Liam stepped forward, both fists clenched against his skinny thighs. He took a couple of shaky breaths before he met Sue's gaze.

"Yes ma'am, I was."

"So you know how the ship works," Sue said. "Your father can't have gone far, and he has to be on board somewhere. We'll get this figured out. Is your mother off shift yet?"

Too late, Sue noticed Evans's wide eyes and shake of his head.

"My birth-mother lives in another pod, ma'am." Liam's face turned red, but he didn't look away from Sue. "They weren't bonded. Only assigned to each other until I was born."

Sue had heard of such arrangements, one of many ways humans dealt with generations spent on board a massive, sprawling ship in deep space.

In love or not, the species had to continue.

She wondered sometimes if assigned mating wasn't easier than trying to manage a bonded relationship long enough to have children, much less raise them.

Most of the time, she was thankful to be years past such concerns.

"Don't worry, Liam, we'll find you somewhere to stay for now. Or someone to stay with you. Did your father say anything about where he'd be? What he was going to be doing today?"

Liam kicked his soft boots against the gray carpeted floor.

"It's his leisure day. Or at least it was." Liam held his breath for a second, then went on in a rush. "But he never did come home last night, ma'am. I thought he was just working late, so I went to sleep. He wasn't there this morning, either. He goes out after his shift to get supplies sometimes, so he doesn't have to leave our pod early on his leisure day. Then today we were going to...I don't know. Whatever I came up with."

Sue tried not to scowl, but she knew she sucked at keeping her feelings to herself. Especially when she was this strung out.

Of course McHugh was on a leisure day. Even during an emergency, the crew took their regulation time off if they possibly could. At least they were supposed to, not following Sue's rotten example. McHugh had missed enough of his leisure days that this one was mandatory, no matter how many lights flashed orange and yellow and thankfully not red under Sue's fingers.

If McHugh had been on duty, she would have had him racing around with everyone else verifying these damn false alarms. She hadn't seen him all day.

And if McHugh had been on duty, missing his much-needed leisure day or not, this frightened boy would know where his father was.

"Good, we can start with that." Sue couldn't stop herself from glancing at the console. Steady for the moment. "Evans, why don't the two of you figure out what supplies McHugh might have been after? What he and Liam were due in the food rotation. We can go from there. Do you need anything right now, Liam? Anything we can get you?"

Liam pressed his lips together until they turned white, but that didn't stop his chin from trembling.

"We were…we always get frozen chocolate, ma'am. On my dad's leisure days. It's his favorite."

"I'll make sure there's some waiting, then," Sue said. "For when he's back with you."

Evans nodded, and she knew he hadn't missed the first clue. The tropical pod on the far edge of *Bellagos*, where the high humidity, temperature, and light wouldn't disturb any other growing pod or lifepod.

The only source for real chocolate on board.

The surrounding pods grew the best ingredients for frozen confections, a staple of human diets even light years away from Earth. Herbs and spices, roots and nuts for smooth, sweet flavors. Every kind of fruit they could manage to bring along did double duty.

Feeding the colonists on the way to seeding the colony.

Sue's overheated brain brought the pathetic contents of her own food stores forward, the lack of any kind of stress-relieving high-calorie treat flashing as bright as her consoles. When she thought back to the last time she'd remembered to eat, she realized that might account for part of her unruly belly.

"Know what?" she said. "If you can hang on for a few minutes, I'll call in my second-in-command. I'm long overdue for a break, and I'm out of just about everything that's fun to eat myself. How about if we talk while we walk over there together?"

Chapter 3

Tima Chou, Sue's second, had been all too happy to step in for as long as she was needed despite her own ongoing efforts to quiet the emergency. Unlike Sue, Tima's short black hair was gleaming and perfectly styled against her head, her uniform clean and unwrinkled. Her second-in-command had shown up so fast Sue wondered if she'd been hovering, waiting for this chance to prove herself in a difficult situation.

Much like Sue had been decades ago when she'd first started getting these opportunities for herself.

Sue did her best to hide her watering eyes from Evans and Liam as they stepped into the bright transit corridors. The curving walls and ceilings were wide enough to let several people walk by in different directions, with the source of that light invisible to anyone who hadn't engineered it.

Same with the source of fresh, almost sweet-smelling air, as if a cleansing rainstorm had recently passed through *Bellagos* unnoticed.

Right now the corridors were awash in the warm yellow of the Earth sun in the early morning hours, the cycle still matching the planet they were leaving farther behind with each passing second. People even picked up a healthy amount of Vitamin D from exposure, something Sue suspected she was lacking, as usual.

As *Bellagos* reached the halfway point on the decades-long journey from Earth to Junos 7, the light cycle would begin the shift to the longer, dimmer day on their new home.

Another lack made itself known in her stiff legs and back. She managed not to walk hunched over, forcing herself into a relatively normal healthy stride to keep up with Evans and Liam. Still, every step, even on the soft, resilient brown surface of the corridor, highlighted how much she'd been working over the past few days.

Well, Sue could be honest with herself even if she ignored both her human and electronic physical monitors' scolding. She'd underworked her body as badly as she'd overworked her mind, fighting that damn corrupted update from Earth HQ with no end in sight.

She hoped her optimism in leaving wouldn't turn out to be misplaced. The slowdown in systems tripping into Alert still held steady, so walking away for a bit shouldn't be a problem. Sue fought to keep her mind off how many of Invalids would await her attention when they returned.

This little boy needed his father, who most certainly should not be in Invalid status.

And Sue desperately did *not* need a mystery disappearance onboard.

She kept half an ear on Evans talking to Liam, the tech's slow, musical drawl only occasionally interrupted by the boy's higher voice. She knew without asking that Evans was recording the conversation like *Bellagos* normally tracked all crew movements, and making mental notes to himself about who else they could assign to search for the missing Mr. McHugh.

A fragment of conversation drifted back to her, mainly because both Liam and then Evans glanced over their shoulders at her. "…short cut, but not right now."

Evans grinned at Sue with a brief shake of his head. She snorted.

If anyone on her security crew could calm Liam down enough to get him to help the investigation, her bet was on Evans.

The thought of a shortcut was anything but calming. *Bellagos* was confusing enough to navigate through official pathways with lighting and signs.

As far as Sue was concerned, getting off the normal paths and into the sections rarely used for anything but maintenance was a fool's game.

A handful of people joined them in the corridor, with only a few jogging in the center lane reserved for them. Not nearly the crowd that would surge out of the various pods at the end of the typical duty cycle for an evening stroll.

Even when given total flexibility in their waking, sleeping, and working hours, a remarkable number of humans went for the standard.

Liam's voice, raised in childlike excitement, caught all of Sue's attention.

"The forest pods are my favorite. They smell like *everything*, and the breeze is a lot stronger. My dad said…" He paused, taking a deep breath. "They say some places on Earth still have forests big enough you can walk across them for days."

"I've seen it myself," Evans said. "Back in the Georgia Zone where I was born. Used to be more city than forest, but they've fixed it all back up now that so many humans are moving off-planet. You could walk for days until you get clear to the ocean."

"The ocean," Liam whispered. "I just can't imagine all that water."

Sue nodded. "That's where I was born. Not in the Georgia Zone, but farther north in the Commonwealth Zone. The water goes on forever it seems, so far you can't see the end of it. Has waves in it, too."

"Like the ones I make when I get to go to the swimming pool?"

"Sure, kind of like that," Evans said, smiling at Sue. "But these move all by themselves without a person or a machine making them. Tides, they're called. The Moon makes them when it goes around and around the Earth."

Liam sighed. "I wish I could have seen the Moon. With my own eyes, on Earth, I mean. Video isn't like the real thing."

"No, it's not." Sue wondered, not for the first time, if it wouldn't be better for these kids to be born once they reached Junos 7. Even if it did make crew numbers pretty much impossible to maintain. "But Junos 7 has three moons, and you'll see those."

The boy shrugged. Sue turned her head so he wouldn't see her pursing her lips. Liam might see those moons as an old man. Neither she nor the much younger Evans would. McHugh wouldn't have either.

No, McHugh *wouldn't*.

Sue refused to let herself slip into past tense, even in her mind, and even when thinking of their eventual deaths in deep space. Not exactly the conversation to have with a scared little boy who simply wanted his father.

Thankfully Evans rescued her.

"Smell that, Liam? I think that's the tropical pod, don't you?"

Sue lifted her nose when the other two did, and the change itself made her feel better. More alert. Instead of clean but recycled air of the corridors on the huge ship, she smelled green and growing things. Sweet and spicy flowers, pungent soil and fertilizer.

The air felt different as they walked closer, too. Warmer, definitely more humid. Full of life in a way she knew she didn't have the words for, but her nose and body recognized.

As they walked through the next curve, Liam's face lit up in a huge grin.

There were surprisingly few signs in the corridors since everyone alive on most of the ship had seen or helped build and connect each new pod.

But the supply pods were different.

To the right, a bold, black-lettered sign in several primary languages and stylized pictograms declared they would find Tropics and Warm Exotics. To the left, Cold and Frozen Supplies. The two opposite pods might appear to be side by side, but past these few meters of corridor, the pods were separated by the void of deep space.

"Frozen chocolate?" Sue said. "That's your dad's favorite?"

Liam's smile faded, but didn't disappear. "Yeah, it's what he always gets on his leisure day. He says we can't keep it around all the time or he'll eat too much of it."

"I'm the same way with anything cherry flavored," Evans said. "I think I'll get some right now, though."

They stepped inside the open portal door that was wide enough to let the three of them walk through together. No one waited inside the white-walled room except three bored attendants. The walls were livened up by larger-than-life display models of everything in stock, along with Earth photos of winter or the frozen Polar Zones. A row of boxy white chairs lined both walls, ready for the much busier strolling hour this evening.

Thank goodness this room was only a couple of degrees

cooler than the rest of *Bellagos* instead of the painful cold of the storage areas.

A young woman with a bouncy brunette ponytail, wearing the pale blue uniform of this zone, brightened when she saw the three of them. Sue thought it was just typical sales behavior—no different here than back on Earth—until the woman focused on the boy.

"Hey there, Liam! Haven't seen you in ages. Where's your dad?"

Chapter 4

SUE DIDN'T HAVE to look to know Evans was making his wide-eyed caution gestures, but he was too late. Liam tried to be brave again, smiling with his chin quivering. He finally leaned forward, holding his belly against the sobs.

"It's okay," Sue said when she saw the woman's stricken face. "You didn't know and we didn't get a chance to warn you."

When Evans touched Liam's shoulder, Liam charged forward for a hug so fast that Evans staggered backward a step. The two of them barely made it to the chairs.

"What happened?" the woman said. Sue finally had a chance to look at her name on the uniform. *Cassie* said. "I didn't mean to upset the poor kid."

Sue shook her head. "*You* didn't upset him. When did you last see Liam and his father?"

The two other attendants wandered over, another young woman and a young man. Cassie turned to them, but they both shook their heads.

"On his last leisure day," she said, frowning. "Seems like

that was a long time ago, though. Did he miss some of them?"

Sue closed her eyes, surprised at how hard that guilt hit. She'd never thought twice about forcing McHugh, Evans, or anyone else to miss their leisure days. Probably because it never crossed her mind to worry about missing her own.

"We've been pretty busy in Systems and Security lately. McHugh was fine just over twelve hours ago. Liam wanted some frozen chocolate, and we needed to ask around. Seemed like a good reason to get a bit of exercise."

Cassie glanced at the other two attendants before stepping closer to Sue.

"Is something going on with the ship, Chief? We've been having trouble with our systems here, and suppliers coming in are saying the same thing. Most people are afraid to ask what's wrong. Is *Bellagos* in trouble?"

Sue took a deep breath, wishing she could get a full sleep cycle before she answered Cassie's questions. It would have been tough enough to explain how a crew member could go missing on a ship in deep space. Sue had been too busy and buried in her systems nightmare to realize people onboard outside of Security knew what was happening.

"We're adjusting from a new systems update from Earth HQ," she said, knowing it wouldn't be enough. "A few hiccups, nothing to worry about."

Cassie stared at Sue for a few seconds, then shook her head.

"Nothing to worry about. Sure. Our monitors are glitchy and unreliable, something happened to this poor kid's father, and our suppliers are fighting every bit as hard to keep conditions in their pods stable as we are. Okay then."

She closed her eyes and lowered her head for a few seconds. When she looked back up and smiled—so fast her ponytail bounced again—Sue would have sworn Cassie had rebooted her own internal system.

"What can we get for you? I bet Liam wants frozen chocolate. How about for you and your friend?"

Sue blinked, trying to get her sluggish and yet anxious mind to function. What kind of frozen treat *did* she like?

"Evans likes cherry," she finally managed. "I'm not sure what…can you just mix them? Cherry and chocolate?"

Cassie smiled, and Sue was surprised to see it looked genuine.

"That's my favorite way to do it. Three double scoops, coming right up, Chief."

Sue waited for a second, but all three of the attendants vanished through the door to the freezer compartment. Probably to get away from the crying little boy and the grumpy security chief.

She sat beside Liam, who was now down to sniffing and trying to catch his breath.

"I'm sorry about that," she said. "You okay, Liam?"

He nodded before he spoke.

"I'm okay, ma'am. I just miss my dad. I wish he was here."

Sue sighed, staring at the blue carpet rather than at the little boy.

She wished McHugh were here, too.

"Where else do you usually go on leisure days?" she said, turning back to Liam. His eyes were red, but he looked calmer. "Is there anyone who your dad knows that you think we should talk to? Or some kind of supplies you were supposed to go get, after your treat?"

A buzz from her wrist comm had Sue back on her feet in an instant.

Tima, her second, reporting another crew member missing, from a couple of hours after McHugh had disappeared. Flipped over to that disturbing Invalid status.

Crew numbers down to eight thousand seven hundred fifty-two.

She looked up to tell Evans to look for connections—well, to bark orders at him, to be honest—but the words died when she saw the horrified, wide-eyed look on Evans's face.

And the frightened look on Liam's.

"I'm sorry," she said. "Wrist comm startled me."

She forced herself to sit again, but the trembling from a jolt of over-stimulated and under-slept bodily systems had already set in. Sue knotted her fingers together in her lap and concentrated on Liam.

He swallowed hard. The obvious movement in his slender neck might have been funny if Sue hadn't been feeling so guilty.

"We were low on protein," he said in a quiet voice. "The meat kind, not the bean kind. I like the meat kind better."

Sue nodded. "I do, too. I'm probably low on that myself. Maybe we can head over after we finish our treats if you're feeling up to it."

She was thankful Evans didn't get the chance to jump in with one of his Old Earth history tidbits about where meat protein used to come from. Cassie walked out then carrying a platform with three transparent cups, gleaming metal spoons standing straight up in the middle of each. One was full of dark brown frozen chocolate, another with dark red cherry. The third held a striped mixture of red and brown.

Cassie still had her bright customer service smile, but Sue thought her eyes were strained and overly bright.

"Here you go! This should get you fixed right up until you find your dad, Liam."

Sue took her bowl, hoping her smile looked at least a little natural. The surface was the same temperature as the room, not cold like she expected. She held it up to the light. Two layers, with a tiny space for air in between.

"Does everything look okay?" Cassie said, a furrow on her smooth brow.

"It looks great," Sue said. "I was just thinking I'd love to have some of these bowls for my place. Do they work for hot things, too?"

"They work fine for hot," Cassie said. "But there are better designs for that. You're better off picking them up at the supply pods. Ours all have tracking units embedded in them."

Liam nodded, taking a few seconds to finish his huge spoonful.

"Yeah, I know all about that. I accidentally walked out with mine, a long time ago when I was little. Big loud alarms went off."

"That's right," Cassie said. "I remember when that happened. Good thing we're all too old for things like that now."

She smiled again, then turned fast enough that her pony-tail whipped out behind her.

Sue finally got a spoonful of her own concoction. Rich dark chocolate and sweet-tart cherry, perfectly balanced. She closed her eyes and sighed, ship and personnel troubles forgotten for one blissful second.

"Good, isn't it?" Evans said. He'd already eaten most of his, and his words sounded like his tongue was half-frozen. It and his lips were dark red. "Everything grown or produced here on *Bellagos*. Nothing dried or frozen from Earth at all now."

"Don't worry about the bowls." Liam's tongue and lips were chocolate brown. "You just leave them on the counter and you won't get in any trouble."

Sue took another huge mouthful. This was nice and all,

but she really should check in. Another missing crewmember, no sign of McHugh, and who knows how many more problems from that Earth update.

She abruptly stood and walked toward the exit.

"Chief?" Evans called. "You okay?"

Sue ignored him, pausing for a second before she stepped across the threshold. She didn't realize how much she'd tensed up for Liam's big loud alarms.

Nothing happened.

She took several steps just to be sure, but still.

Silence.

Her mind was weary and overstressed, but Sue saw the row of orange and yellow alerts back in her command pod clearly before she even pulled out her comm. Not one of them was for the tracking systems on board.

Those were green all across, or they had been when she left Tima in command.

Evans stood at the edge of the pod, managing to look puzzled and worried at the same time. Liam waited behind him, eyes wide.

"Go on," Sue said. "Try it. Make sure there's not some fluke with mine, or interference from my comm or me."

Evans shrugged and stepped over, and Sue saw his shoulders relax when everything stayed silent. They both turned and waved Liam forward.

The boy stuck his toe over, then slowly held the bowl out. At the continued lack of big loud alarms, he grinned and scooted over to Sue and Evans.

"It's turned off," Liam said, scraping the bottom of his bowl. "We could take all kinds of things with us!"

Sue raised one eyebrow and met Evans's gaze.

"No alarms on the tracking sensors," she said. "They show all green."

"But something's wrong," he said. "Might be time for that reboot."

"And switch out to the old systems if we can force the rollback. Looks like we're about to get in trouble, alarms or not."

They all turned to see Cassie and the other two workers staring at them, arms crossed and nearly identical frowns on their faces.

"We better take these back in," Liam whispered, but he was still smiling. "Or they might not serve us next time."

Chapter 5

A CLOSER READ of Tima's message about the new missing crewmember alert had Sue detouring them all away from her command center and back toward the protein pods after all.

"You're sure?" Evans said, trying to keep his voice too low for Liam to hear. "The missing woman was going to the same place McHugh was?"

Sue nodded, smiling when Liam glanced back at them.

"Last time she checked in with her partner, that's where she was headed. Restock on protein. The meat kind."

"And we still can't check video."

"Nope. Not until Earth HQ says I can roll back that update and get us onto a reliable systems suite. Nothing new has gone orange for what, an hour now? We should be able to roll back the second I get the all clear in a few hours."

The protein pods were only one corridor away from the frozen pods, or else Sue would have passed this off to someone else. At least that's what she told herself.

The truth was she felt certain this would turn out to be important. Too important to leave to anyone else, no matter how itchy she got about the botched update and waiting for Earth HQ.

The entrance looked similar to the one they'd just left, with the two protein pods splitting off the main corridor. In this case, the signs showed that the growing pod off to the left held soybeans, peanuts, and even a few species of tree nuts that had been modified to thrive when kept short and compact.

The pod off to the right was just as interesting in the opposite way.

That one was row after row of vats, most of them too regulated and carefully controlled to allow for visitors. A few were maintained out front for educational purposes, so youngsters like Liam could see where their protein came from.

And older crewmembers could be reassured that it no longer came from living creatures somehow confined and hidden away onboard *Bellagos*.

Only the cellular descendants from the original tissue samples taken over a century ago from some of the last farmed cattle, chicken, fish, and other creatures had made this trip.

The pod looked similar to the frozen treat one they'd just left, with bright white walls and photographs of what was available for residents of *Bellagos*. Images of prepared dishes rather than the source of the protein, of course. A row of the educational, smaller versions of the grow tanks lined one wall, their green walls contrasting with the vivid reds, pinks, and whites of the growing protein. The attendants even wore similar cheerful uniforms and friendly smiles.

But Sue saw even more strain and worry behind those smiles than she had with Cassie.

One of them who wasn't smiling stepped forward, a

stone-faced gray-haired man about Sue's age. She had her protein and most other supplies delivered when she remembered to get food at all, so she only vaguely recognized him.

Quite handsome, really, if in a mildly intimidating way.

"Chief Warrell. We've been expecting you. Dan Greenwell."

He didn't offer his hand, only stood with his arms crossed.

"Expecting me, huh? Evans, why don't you and Liam go take a look at those tanks?" Sue waited for Evans to nod and for him and Liam to walk to the farthest tank. "Exactly why were you expecting me?"

Greenwell shrugged, shaking his head.

"Our first contact today was with the young woman's partner, wondering if she'd been here. She hadn't. This was after we've been fighting with our systems and tanks for three solid days. The only way anyone could disappear from *Bellagos* would be some kind of systems error. Thus, we were expecting you."

"Fair enough. Are you familiar with Senior Tech Andy McHugh, or his son Liam?" She jerked her chin at the boy.

"Sure, I know Liam," Greenwell said, nodding. "Haven't seen Andy in here for a while now."

"Not at all over the past couple of days?"

Greenwell raised his dark eyebrows, a sharp contrast to the gray hair.

"No. I keep special orders for him, the best ground beef we produce. Liam loves an Earth-style hamburger. Probably one of the few *Bellagos*-born who even know what that is. Andy hasn't been in for days. Missing too, is he?"

Sue stared up at the ceiling, then down at the soothing blue carpet. She wished she *could* call in a separate Security unit on this and get back to her own domain. She wasn't cut out for this kind of face-to-face work, for deciding in the moment what to tell and what to keep to herself.

In the first decade of this mission, neither she nor anyone else had had any need for more security than what the tracking systems and vids provided.

"Like you said, Mr. Greenwell, no one can actually disappear from the ship. We just need to locate them. You seem to have thought a lot about this. If they never got here when people expected them to, where do you think they might have gotten…dislocated? Any ideas?"

He shook his head slowly, never looking away from Sue's eyes.

"My only idea would be to check the vids. Systems and Security knows where every one of us is at all hours, in case we need help of some kind. That's what all those recordings are *supposed* to be for, right?"

Sue took a deep breath, wishing again for a full sleep cycle. She wasn't yet sure if Mr. Greenwell would prefer to be on her side or not. Either way, he was too quick for her to deal with in her stim-weary state.

Might as well try to sway the balance to her side.

"That is indeed what the recordings are for, Mr. Greenwell. As I'm sure you already suspect, the systems problems are keeping us from accessing those for the moment. May I ask what your background is? What did you do back on Earth?"

He smiled with half his face, as if the other half was unable—or unwilling—to shed the stony expression.

"Have I been a tank wrangler all my life, you mean? No. My family was in that line of work, some of the first to pioneer tank-grown protein back in the old days. I went into the military instead, then law enforcement."

"Systems and Security didn't try to recruit you?"

Dan Greenwell finally smiled all the way. Sue was

surprised at how the hard planes and angles of his face were transformed into warm and welcoming by a simple movement of his facial muscles.

"They did. Earth HQ still sends a new and improved offer every few months. They can't quite seem to understand that I did my time and was ready to move on to something else. *Somewhere* else. If I'd wanted to stay in my old line of work, I would have stayed on Old Earth."

Sue laughed at that, doing her best to keep it quiet so Liam wouldn't hear. Greenwell had just about repeated her reasons for joining this mission. She suspected he was another like her, unattached and past the time for adding to the ship's population, and certain to die before they ever reached their destination.

And as unable to resist the adventure as she was.

"I can't argue," she said. "You sound a lot like me. I won't try to recruit you, but I may want to ask you more questions at some point. I spend too much time cooped up in my command pod to know what's going on in people's lives. With your background and training, I'd bet *you* know more than you let on."

Dan tilted his head forward in an oddly old-fashioned half bow, half acknowledgement.

"I admit I pay attention to folks. One of those lifelong habits that was impossible to leave behind. I'll help if I can. Ask anytime. But you know better than I do that nothing's likely to get sorted out until you can get a good look at those recordings."

This time he did hold out his hand, and Sue was surprised at how warm and pleasant it was to touch another person. Especially when Dan Greenwell held on a bit longer than strictly necessary.

She *did* spend too much time isolated in that command pod.

"I'll take you up on that offer, then," Sue said. "We could have some kind of serious issue with the ship itself, doors getting jammed or something like that, but Maintenance isn't reporting anything. I'll admit to you for your ears only that I noticed a sensor anomaly over at the frozen treats pod just now. It could be that simple."

"But the people are actually missing," Dan said. "Like Liam's father. So either we have crewmembers getting trapped by the ship…"

"Or they're getting trapped by other crewmembers. Have you heard any chatter along those lines? Someone upset enough to consider something like this? Someone you felt like you should be paying closer attention to?"

Dan rubbed his chin, watching Liam and Evans.

"For your ears only, right?" He waited for Sue to nod. "We're not the only ones to notice problems with ship systems. That's unsettling the crew more than I'd like. Unsettled people behave in predictable and unpredictable ways. None of them good."

"Understood," Sue said. "Anything before the systems trouble? I don't have suspects before you ask, but I need to know what we may be dealing with."

"I do hear rumblings here and there, but nothing more serious than what young people generally get up to. I'm sure you know the kind. Barely grown up enough to know they're not kids anymore, not quite grown up enough to have any sense."

"I know the type. I distantly remember *being* the type."

"Yeah, me too," Dan said with another of those brilliant smiles. "Dealt with them a lot over the years. No one onboard got my attention enough to report to the good people over at Systems and Security."

"Fair enough," she said. "If memory serves, it's a lot more

talk than action. We're planning to reboot and try to bring the recordings up as soon as we can. I'll be in touch."

He flashed that smile again. "Good."

Sue did her best to ignore Evans and his raised eyebrows and grin as they left.

Chapter 6

NONE of the yellow Invalid systems had flashed back over to orange by the time Sue got back to her chilly, cramped command pod. Tima reassured her that no new orange lights had popped up, either.

But Tima's fidgety stance and restless eyes gave the bad news away before she'd finished talking.

Three more crew members had shown up missing. And Invalid.

Eight thousand seven hundred forty-nine, when there should be eight thousand seven hundred fifty-four.

As soon as Tima left, Sue slapped the command override for silence and no interruptions into effect again, relieved a thousand times over that she'd sent Evans off-duty to take Liam home to his own pod for the night-cycle.

A boy that age didn't need to stay alone, or hear the words she muttered as she read the crewmember notes.

Nothing in common in the two men and one woman who had now vanished into thin, cleaned, and re-circulated air. Only that they'd all disappeared during the last twelve hours. And the Invalid status flashing next to their names, along with the others.

Sue leaned forward, letting her command chair carry her the rest of the way. A quick comm to each reporting family member verified what she'd suspected but refused to assume.

All three had been on their way to the protein pod. The meat kind.

She let out one last string of obscenities for the moment. Sure, she'd meant to get back in touch with Dan Greenwell. She'd even been looking forward to it. But not today, barely an hour after she'd met him.

And not with news like this.

News that had her suspecting she needed to *question* him rather than ask him questions.

A scroll and a few taps, and his handsome face filled her view screen. He even smiled.

"Chief Warrell. Glad to see you again, but I'm afraid it can't be good news so quickly."

"No, Mr. Greenwell, it's not. We've had three more reports come in. All missing. All headed your way. I need to ask if any of them actually made it there."

He listened intently as she gave names and descriptions, his brown eyes narrowed in concentration. He leaned to the side for a second, accessing his own systems.

"I don't recall any of them being here over the last few days, and they're not showing up in our records, either."

Sue rubbed her face. "Okay. I'm going to check from here, but do you have any thoughts on what they could have in common? From those stubborn habits of yours? There are five of them now."

"Nothing jumps to mind, no. I'll run their records to make sure."

Sue nodded, thinking of a thousand questions she could ask someone with a career in law enforcement. She was an outstanding troubleshooter, and she knew every single system on this ship inside and out. Hell, she'd installed more than a few of them.

But she had no training and hardly any experience in investigating people.

The mission planners had optimistically assumed demand for such investigations would be low to none with so much surveillance on board.

Surveillance that was still locked out.

"Great," she said. "Thank you. Let me know if you find anything, or think of anything. I'll do the same."

Dan smiled again, and despite her anxiety, Sue smiled back. He only said one word.

"Good."

Sue scrubbed her fingers through her hair, recognizing the start of one of the other annoying side-effects from prolonged use of stims. Her scalp itched horribly, and she knew her back, palms, and toes would be next.

Still, the combination of a walk in the programmed sunlight and a good dose of ice cream had cleared her thinking enough to do something besides fight alert status lights.

She checked the time of her last transmission to Earth HQ. Still half the day cycle before she could expect a reply, and that was assuming they'd replied right away rather than meeting and discussing and wasting time debating every possible action and outcome. Sue had been part of all that and more with this mission's planning and startup, to the point that she'd been tempted to deliberately break the communications systems after launch.

But until now, the Earth HQ updates had made her job and her life easier, every single time. Those programmers— safely on the birthplace of humanity rather than out here expanding its boundaries—had time to analyze and improve the software more than she ever would.

With five crewmembers missing but presumably still alive, she was willing to give HQ that time to respond. Unless the situation here out on the boundary worsened.

She pulled up all five of the missing crew members on her main screen, including Liam McHugh's father.

Not a thing in common, just as she suspected. McHugh in Systems and Security, the others in Physical Maintenance, Medical, Entertainment, and Horticultural. Each a vital department and job in their own way, especially for thousands of humans spending entire lifetimes inside a massive spaceship. All of them from different sections of the living pods.

No reason Sue could see that each of them would turn up missing. No reason *any* of them would.

That sensor in the frozen treats pod was damn strange, too. She couldn't quite put it out of her mind.

Liam's face flashed into her mind, and not the worried or sad version. This one was more like a typical little boy, with a broad smile and sparkling eyes.

He'd been walking with Evans in front of her, crossing the rounded intersections from one pod branch to another. Liam had said something low, clearly meant for Evans and not her.

Something about…a shortcut.

Sue pulled up a map of *Bellagos*, then zoomed in and tapped the home location for each missing person. No pattern there, only scattered random dots. She zoomed out, located the supply pods, and highlighted the protein pods.

Her mind traced the routes like a decision tree in a systems schematic.

Finally, something she could at least investigate.

Chapter 7

Bellagos has been built in orbit around Earth, with massive sections assembled and hauled into place over several years. Some sections like spokes in a wheel, some long tubes. Others bulky square or rounded shapes that joined the rest together.

Environmental and health engineers had designed corridors that were broad and inviting to connect the main sections of the ship. Like the ones Sue had walked through with Liam and Evans today, they held simulated sunlight and sometimes even birdsongs or breezes.

They were also designed to help crewmembers get a big part of their exercise needs by walking or running from the living pods to work, play, or gather supplies.

Sue kept to the designated corridors like most other crewmembers. Not because of some long-buried desire to follow the rules.

Sue only followed the rules that suited her or the ones that made things easier.

Keeping to the corridors was definitely the latter.

To her, the idea of wandering around in the old junctions

—used for construction and maintenance but otherwise empty—held no appeal whatsoever. They were utilitarian to the point of being unpleasant. Bare steel surfaces, lighting either dim or glaring. Not well-ventilated or overly clean, full of the odd creaks and groans of *Bellagos* talking to herself.

Sue hated to admit it, but those echoing, dim spaces went beyond lonely and deserted. They were downright creepy.

But on the tracking displays, she'd noticed several crewmembers passing through those old passageways. Including one that led from several of the living pod wings to the supply wings, cutting off the longer and far more pleasant main corridor.

Was that what happened here?

Had the corrupted systems update turned the shortcuts into the trap Sue had always worried they could be?

She saw Liam and Evans in her mind again, looking back over their shoulders at her and grinning.

Sue sat up, her heart pounding faster than even her over-abundance of stims could account for, moving faster than the chair could compensate for. She scrolled through the comm and keyed her emergency code.

"Damnit Evans, report. Report!"

After a couple of minutes of what would be a piercing alarm in a small living pod, Sue ended the comm.

She couldn't remember ever shying away from a report or a survey or facing an angry superior in her entire career. Her whole life, really. She hadn't thought it was in her DNA to put off an unpleasant thing she'd have to face later on.

But Sue's hand shook when she reached toward the ship status console.

Personnel tracking. Crew count.

The already missing had the count down to eight thousand seven hundred forty-nine.

And the current count had it down to eight thousand seven hundred forty-seven.

Sue knew what she would see, but she had to confirm it for herself.

Both Liam and Evans with Invalid yellow flashing under their names.

She jumped so hard the seat jerked and tried to compensate when an emergency status comm rang through. Sue hit accept without caring who it was for a change.

"Chief Warrell, Dan Greenwell here." His face, back to its usual stony visage, fell into a frown when he saw her. "What's happened? You're paler than you were before."

"We're up to…up to seven missing now, Mr. Greenwell." Sue took a deep breath. "Why don't you tell me why you used emergency status before I say any more? And how the hell you have an emergency status code to begin with."

Dan's face relaxed into a tiny smile with one raised eyebrow.

"Earth HQ pushed it on me, to be honest. Someone there couldn't tolerate such a distinguished and decorated veteran or some such nonsense not having some kind of special privileges. Never used it before. I'd never planned to, either, had to look the code up just now."

"Because…"

"Because the two crewmembers who are supposed to be on shift now haven't reported in. I know, I know, a couple of kids barely an hour late isn't cause to be interrupting you with everything else going on. But you did say to let you know if my stubborn instincts kicked in. They just did."

Sue opened her mouth to ask for names and where the two lived, but a change on the ship status console caught her eye.

"Would those two missing kids happen to be Charlie Haslett and Debora Hahn?"

Dan's face switched to a full-on scowl. Sue knew anyone who'd run across that look in his former military or law enforcement lives would have had good reason to be scared half to death.

"Care to tell me exactly how you knew that? They both live alone, no one to report them missing but me."

"They just switched to Invalid status on my end. Listen, can you meet me now? I need to check something out, and I could use your instincts on this one if you're willing."

"You bet. Just tell me where and when. This horseshit has gone on long enough."

Sue told him the intersection she'd pinpointed earlier, the one between the living pods and his protein supply pod. She wasn't sure whether she liked his decidedly Old Earth swearing or the fierce light in his brown eyes more.

"Got it. Need me to bring anything else?" he said.

"I'm calling in someone from Maintenance and someone from the Security side to meet us. Bring your old habits and we should be just fine."

Sue made one more call before she headed out, and just as she'd hoped, Tima Chou was outside the door before Sue opened it. A crowd of people passed back and forth behind her, strolling and chatting.

A crowd that was only going to get bigger as the evening cycle wore on, and possibly make the number of missing and Invalid bigger, too.

"Chief! There aren't more missing?"

"There are, Tima. I'm heading out to meet Maintenance to see if we can get ahead of this before it gets worse." Sue checked the time on her comm. "We're down to within an hour of the window for hearing back from Earth HQ, assuming they're not hashing this out in an endless bullshit meeting. You prepared for that?"

Tima's restless motion vanished, and she stood at rigid attention.

"You bet I am, Chief. What are your orders?"

"Watch ship status for more…"

Sue stared, eyes unfocused, over-stimmed mind jittering and yelling at her to not walk away. Not yet!

Not until she made the rest of *Bellagos* as safe as she possibly could without the risky reboot.

Tima jumped out of the way as Sue ducked back into her command pod.

She keyed in the emergency ship-wide address code she'd never expected to use.

Anyone who wasn't sound asleep would see the words on all comms and screens, hear her voice on all ship audio systems. Even the ones sleeping would get the recorded alert as soon as they woke.

"This is Systems and Security Chief Warrell. Effective immediately, all crewmember access to unauthorized passageways on *Bellagos* is forbidden until further notice. I say again, all access to unauthorized passageways on *Bellagos* is forbidden. Any attempt to enter these passageways without my direct permission will be punished with confinement to quarters and restriction to basic food rations."

She followed that up by restricting access to all Maintenance areas onboard, again to levels she'd never expected to use. Now only the two Maintenance crewmembers she was meeting were cleared for access. No one else—working in Maintenance and normally cleared—would be able to go in or out without pinging Sue's own wrist comm.

She stepped back out into the corridor, unruly belly knotting as her own voice echoed all around her.

The busy crowd stopped, staring at their wrist comms and each other.

Tima stared wide-eyed at Sue, but she only said one word.

"Understood."

Sue nodded once.

"Honestly, that should do it. Still, watch for crew members to flip to Invalid. I hope not, but humans have been known to do crazier things. Now, if I give the word, are you willing to shut down all systems and reboot? No matter what my status shows, or what you hear from Earth HQ?"

Tima stared up at Sue with unblinking brown eyes. Sue would have sworn the girl—correction, young woman—vibrated with energy and indecision.

Tima was more of a rule-follower than Sue had ever been.

Despite Sue's best efforts to train that out of her.

"Yes, Chief. You're highest on any chain of command out here. Give the word, and it's done."

"Good. If that crew number count changes or you hear from Earth HQ, I want to hear it from you before anyone else. Otherwise, I trust your judgment to act as needed. You should too. Okay. Here's what I'm going to try."

Chapter 8

Sue worked her way through the streams of nervous and chattering walkers, continuing her best efforts not to meet anyone's eyes. Her habit of overwork and basically avoiding people on the few hours she had off was paying off beautifully, with no one recognizing her.

If one person managed to remember her face from some long-ago command list, she knew everyone would swarm her with questions she was in no position to answer. Especially with no sleep and the stim-itch flaring up like mad. It was everything she could do to stop herself from digging at her palms or stopping to scratch her back against the corridor wall.

A faster walk than she thought possible had her leaving the spotless white corridor with light changing to the warm, reddish glow of evening behind. The floor was bare, bone-jarring steel instead of springy carpeting. Rather than curving and welcoming, the walls of this junction met at hard right angles, and the white was more utilitarian, almost grubby.

Sue doubted any of the Health and Morale engineers had given a thought to this space.

Mainly because none of the crew were supposed to *be* here besides Maintenance. And then only if they had to be. People standing beside a rectangular doorway set so flat into the wall that it nearly disappeared let her know she was in the right place.

Jacinda Kim was familiar from Sue's own team. Older and more experienced than Tima, but she stood just as rigidly at attention. Sue hated to admit it, but she was relieved to see Jacinda looked as rumpled and tired as she herself felt, with brown circles under her eyes and curly brown hair flattened on one side.

The Maintenance tech, Martinez according to his uniform, waited beside Jacinda. Like her, his wide, black belt had several storage compartments and pouches, and he carried a metallic fabric bag slung over his shoulder. His gleaming bald head didn't reveal whether he'd recently tried to catch a nap, but his expression was attentive. His green eyes secure and confident.

Exactly what Sue needed.

She turned at the echo of boots on the metal floor and was relived to see Dan Greenwell. He'd shed the white service uniform and wore casual pants and shirt in a muted green that suited him better than she wanted to admit.

"Okay, we're all in place," Sue said into her comm. "Any changes?"

"Two more missing, ma'am," Tima's amplified voice replied. "Nowhere near you, though."

"*Damn* it. Understood. Note their records for my follow-up and stand by."

Sue turned to Martinez. "We need to get into the Maintenance area here. I know people use it as a shortcut, and you know crewmembers are going missing. We need to see if those two things are related."

Martinez scowled for a second, rubbing his smooth head.

"I know I don't have clearance to ask this, Chief Warrell. Like you know you don't have clearance to ask me to let all of you into the Maintenance passages without an emergency, especially after you yourself just locked them down. Does this have to do with the systems trouble since the last Earth HQ update?"

Sue met Dan's smiling eyes for a second before she turned to Martinez.

"One thing I've learned over the last few hours is how much everyone outside of Systems and Security knows about operations I thought were secure. At least when they go wrong. Yes, Martinez. This is related to the bad update, and the reason for the lock-down. I'm trying to keep it from getting worse. Right now you and Jacinda are cleared to access Maintenance areas, but no one else."

Martinez stared into her eyes for several seconds, then shrugged and smiled.

"Good enough for me, as long as you don't put me on those nasty basic food rations."

He waved his wrist-comm across the center of the door, counted to three, then pushed it open.

The air in the little-used passage they stood in wasn't kept as fresh and invigorating as in the main corridors, but Sue and everyone else flinched away from a stale mechanical odor that rushed out of the passage, like overused synthetic lubricants and warm plastics.

"Sorry for the stink," Martinez said. "Normally circulation is better than this, even in maintenance passages."

"Your systems have been Invalid for twenty-eight hours," Sue said, amazed at how the accurate number popped so effortlessly into her mind. "It's happening all over the ship."

Sue started forward, then felt a hand on her shoulder. Jacinda Kim's cheeks were flushed, but she held her head high.

"I'm sorry, Chief. You have good reason to suspect a problem here, and I trust good reason to declare these passageways off-limits. That's why you called me. I'm going in first."

Sue stepped back, waving her arm toward the door.

"You and Martinez be my guests to work that out between you." A tingle in the back of Sue's overworked and under-rested brain made her hold up one hand. "Only far enough for us to close the door, then hold there."

Martinez laughed under his breath, but he smiled at Jacinda.

"The shortcut toward the supply pods is to the right. Watch your heads. Lighting should activate with motion, but that's been iffy over the past couple of day cycles."

Jacinda pushed her curls behind her ears and pulled a finger-sized trouble light off her belt. She held her breath, hesitating for only a second before she stepped into the darker passage.

Martinez followed.

Sue spoke into her comm. "We're going in, Tima. Let me know if anything changes on our status."

Sue glanced at Dan. "You willing to go last? See if those old law enforcement skills keep us out of a breakdown or ambush or whatever else we're walking into?"

Dan tilted his head and waved his arm toward the door, much like Sue had done for Jacinda.

"I'll do my best."

Chapter 9

THE OVERHEAD LIGHTS in the passage were barely flickering by the time Sue stepped inside. She hadn't been in the Maintenance areas for years, and she still didn't like them. A narrow and angular hallway stretched on to the left, right, and straight ahead, with walls, floor, and ceiling a dark, non-reflective gray.

When the lights finally managed to stay on at full, harsh brightness, the surfaces seemed to absorb the light so they could hold onto their shadows.

The surface absorbed sound, too, leaving Sue feeling like her ears were stuffed full of cotton. Normal shifting and shuffling noises of four humans crowded together barely registered.

Her flattened sense of hearing only brought the stim-induced ringing in her ears back into her awareness in full unpleasant force.

Martinez sighed and rolled his eyes, tension draining from his body. His scalp reflected more than the walls did.

"I was afraid we were going to make the whole walk in the dark."

Jacinda kept her light in her hand as she stared down the right-side passage, clearly not surprised by the darkness just ahead.

"Listen, Martinez," Sue said. "How are people getting in here? The ones not in Maintenance. Or Security. The way I have access set right now, even how it's normally set, Mr. Greenwell's comm won't let him in, correct?"

Martinez crossed his arms and leaned against the wall.

"That all depends, Chief. From what I hear, crewmembers trade favors to get their comms hacked if they don't know how to do it themselves. That or they follow someone. Or sometimes they just push on every maintenance door until they catch one that's not locked properly."

Sue shook her head, unable to stop a grunt of surprise.

"And how often is this happening? Doors unlocked, or comms hacked?"

Martinez grinned. From the looks of him, he wasn't directly involved in any of the illicit activity. But he wasn't concerned and wasn't afraid to say so.

He shrugged. "We do our best to keep the doors secured. Where we are right now is an access passage. A little dull, not all that dangerous. The deeper you get into the ship—away from the living areas—the more people can get hurt or break things. I honestly don't know much about the comms since I've never hacked one. People taking shortcuts is annoying, but it's never been a real problem before."

Sue peered down the dim central passage in front of them, spotting doorways on both sides before it got too dark to see. The stink of the ship's guts was stronger there, too.

"That sound about right to you?" she said to Dan right beside her. "If there are no problems that you've heard about, leave it alone?"

"Martinez here just described every military base I've ever seen. Every college campus, too, and a hell of a lot of municipal buildings back on Earth. People are going to see how much they can get away with no matter what you do to stop it. I always figured it was better to let the small things go as long as it never escalated."

"Yeah, it all worked fine until the latest great Earth HQ update," Sue said. "Close and secure that door, would you, Martinez?" She waited until he had, then raised her wrist comm. "Still seeing us, Tima?"

The silence stretched on, long enough for Sue to count to twenty.

"I was afraid of that. Okay, Martinez, see if you can get back out."

Martinez blinked, then stepped back over to the door. When his wrist comm didn't work, he moved to the side and held his hand flat against a recessed panel Sue hadn't noticed. He shook his head, but he was reaching for the metallic bag over his shoulder.

"No good, not responding to me at all. I've got the tools to get any door on *Bellagos* open, but anyone outside of Maintenance would have a hell of a time of it."

He pulled out a silvery tool that seemed to have three tiny flattened heads protruding a few centimeters out of a rounded body. He fitted the tool into slots Sue couldn't make out even while she was watching him. One on each side of the door, one top, one bottom, with a muted grinding noise and flashing movement from the ends each time.

The door gave a low thump and slid open.

"Good work," Sue said. "Let's all go back out and see if we still exist."

As soon as she stepped clear of the door, Sue's comm let out the jarring screech of an emergency alert, and Jacinda's did the same. Sue's heart pounded even though she was sure she knew what she was about to hear.

"Tima? What's happening?"

"There you are! You all dropped off, just like you thought."

"But we're back on the status screen now?"

Dan frowned at Sue when several seconds passed before Tima's reply.

"I'm sorry, Chief, but no. All four of you are still showing as Invalid."

"That's why your comm didn't work," Dan said to Martinez. "In theory, I'd guess all access should switch off if something like that happened. Crew members switching to Invalid."

Sue nodded. She rubbed her temples, trying to catch the thoughts her weary mind must have missed earlier. Way back when something as simple as the sensors on her ice cream cup not working seemed like a huge clue, and her biggest concern was dealing with the stim-itch that now crawled across her scalp again.

"I'll have to reset us all if a full system reboot doesn't do it," she said. "But that doesn't explain what's been happening here. Liam McHugh's father has been missing for hours. Now Liam and Evans are, too. None of them instantly tripped into Invalid status. It took time."

"Maybe the changes you made to shipwide access accelerated whatever is happening," Jacinda said.

Sue nodded. "That may be, makes sense. Tima, we're heading back into the shortcut. I need you to verify the last several missing crewmembers. After Evans. I did the first few, but then we all assumed that status was the truth."

"You already said that, Chief," Tima said, "before you headed out. Verified one as missing, another as safe and sound, but in Invalid status. Working on the others. Still no word from Earth HQ. Let me know when…whatever you know."

Sue looked at Dan Greenwell. If she didn't already know,

she would have guessed he had some kind of investigative background by the gleam in his eyes, the flush in his cheeks. He might have been perfectly happy over the last several years working with his protein vats.

But that wasn't what he was *made* for.

"Those old instincts back in gear, Mr. Greenwell?" she said. "Still willing to go with us?"

"Try and stop me. You solved a big part of it, Chief. But something besides faulty sensors is going on here."

Chapter 10

Sᴜᴇ, Dan, and Martinez followed Jacinda back into the Maintenance passage. Jacinda had run her fingers through her hair enough that it wasn't the least bit flat, on the one side or anywhere else. When the door refused to respond to his comm, Martinez used the same whirling gadget to close the door behind them.

They headed deeper into the ship.

Sue remembered from the map that they were cutting off two of the long main corridors, turning an hour's steady walk into about fifteen minutes. But by the time Jacinda gave up on waiting for the motion sensor lights to kick on and charged ahead with her trouble light, Sue was sure they'd been walking for hours.

The wall to the right remained the same unbroken, dull gray, while passage after passage jutted off to the left. Several sloped sharply up or down, and Sue suspected ladders waited just out of sight. Designers of the mechanical areas of *Bellagos* hadn't worried about keeping a level, human-friendly plane like they had for living areas. Certainly not when so much of it was built in orbit with no worries about gravity, artificial or otherwise.

The stink rose and fell as they walked, but never quite disappeared. The lack of sound, from footsteps or breathing or much of anything else, set Sue's nerves on edge. It was everything she could do not to scratch at her scalp and the palms of her hands.

Finally Jacinda stopped, turning around with her light held toward the floor. The overhead lights weren't even flickering, but Sue could see a door behind Jacinda. Their access passage had come to an end.

Martinez stepped forward, waving his wrist comm and touching the recessed panel, then working on the top of the door as he had before.

Nothing happened. He examined the silvery heads, then tried one of the sides. He leaned closer with his own trouble light.

He shook his head and scowled. "This isn't right. Even if my comm is bad, every door on this ship is designed to work with this tool. It's hard to tell without magnification, but I think the access points have been jammed."

"Part of the system update?" Sue said.

"I don't think so." Martinez was rubbing his head again. "The port isn't even engaging. The other door worked fine until the ship thought we disappeared, then I got it open anyway. This one is physically jammed."

Dan turned in a slow circle. "So we, and probably the others, were meant to get in but not get out."

Jacinda joined Dan, shining her light all around them. Nothing but the dark passage they'd come through, the jammed door, and a passage heading off to the left.

"I didn't see the map, Chief," Jacinda said. "And honestly, this isn't one of the passages I normally use. Will anyone hear us if we shout or beat on this door? Out in the main corridor, I mean?"

"I doubt it. This comes out in another one of those side corridors. And if this end has been jammed for a few days, I'd bet people have stopped trying it as a shortcut."

"Someone in *here* might hear us, though," Dan said. "If we're loud enough over this sound damping. Someone we're not ready to meet just yet."

Martinez stowed the door tool back in his pouch and stood with his hands on his hips.

"I can head down any of these other passages and find a way around. Or I can get bigger tools and get us out of here by force. But I have no idea what I'll run into or if I'll make it back out."

"Forget it," Dan said. "We're not splitting up. Either we got funneled down here on purpose and they're hesitating for some reason, or they're busy and not paying attention. We know for certain that at least one person has disappeared from here."

"Probably three," Sue said. "I'm sure this is the shortcut Liam wanted to show Evans."

"Well then," Jacinda said, her voice tight, "we should head back to the door we know is working. Bring a bigger crew back, more Security and more Maintenance. Figure out what the hell is going on."

Dan started to speak, but Sue touched his arm.

"I think we're out of time for that."

Chapter 11

In the horrible silence, a soft shuffling sound grew
steadily louder.

Sue didn't protest when Dan joined her and Jacinda
shoulder to shoulder across the narrow passage in front of the
jammed door. None of them could tell where the noise came
from, but with exactly none of them armed, that didn't seem
to matter much.

Jacinda jerking her light around and Martinez darting his
between their heads only added to the disorientation.

"Whoever it is can only be another crewmember," Dan
said in a low voice. "There are no energy weapons or even
projectile weapons onboard. Not unless someone built
them."

"We have no need for such crude devices," a soft voice
said from somewhere to their right. "One easily jammed
door and human nature are doing everything we need and
more, aren't they?"

Jacinda and a beat later Martinez swung their trouble
lights down the passage. Two men and two women waited,
one of the women out in front. All of them wore leisure

clothing like Dan, soft gray with no rank or name visible. No weapons of any kind visible, either.

Sue didn't recognize them, but she heard and felt Dan let out a breath beside her.

"Mayam," he said. "What's going on here?"

"Where's the boy?" Sue said, stepping forward. "My crew?"

Now that they were only a couple of meters away, Sue could see they were younger than she'd thought. The woman, Mayam, didn't look like she'd reached her second decade. She was tall but not filled out yet, wavy black hair chopped in bunches around her narrow face. Still very much an angular and gawky kid to Sue's eyes.

"*Your* crew, Chief?" Mayam said, shaking her head. "That may be true of the ones who volunteered for this mission. Maybe the ones born here. But not all of us."

Dan raised his hands. "Listen to me. This isn't going to accomplish whatever you want. Especially not holding people against their will."

"What's my other option, then?" Mayam waved an empty hand at Sue. "Petition the warden here for early release? Jump off at the next stop?"

"How will capturing and holding people change any of that?" Sue said. "They can't turn *Bellagos* around any more than I can. Why are you doing this?

Mayam stepped forward until stood almost nose to nose with Sue. At Jacinda's defensive movement to her side, Sue held up her hand.

"This is at least doing *something*!" Mayam shouted, fists clenched in front of her stomach. "Making a decision, having a bloody choice. For the first time in our lives we're not... inert!"

Dan moved toward Sue and a little bit in front of her. Rather than someone trying to downplay her own authority, he was clearly putting on his old role in law enforcement.

And acting on whatever his relationship to this Mayam really was.

"I know you were young when you were brought on board," he said. "Many of you were, long before you could have made such a choice for yourselves. We can't fix it, no. But we can't do anything to help if you keep taking the choices of others away."

"Is the boy safe?" Sue said. "Liam? He was born here, and he loves it here. This is his only home."

Mayam scowled and waved her arm. "Do you think I'm trying to set up some kind of hostage trading program? Keep rounding them up until there aren't enough people left to keep this floating prison ship working?"

"Did you sabotage our systems?" Sue said. "Disable the tracking units in this passageway? I don't remember your name from the list of missing."

Mayam tried to hide it, but a flash of pride lit her eyes. She stepped back and crossed her arms.

"Earth HQ isn't quite as all-powerful as we've been led to believe. That bit wasn't even hard to do. If you check your *infallible* snooping systems, you'll see me and everyone with me still where we're supposed to be. Vital signs, movements, everything. Just like normal."

Sue clenched her fists, surprised at how badly she wanted to use them.

"You're disrupting the lives of everyone on board to do what? Prove a point? What's your next target, Mayam? Life support? I asked you if you sabotaged our systems. I suggest you give me an answer."

"We don't have a death wish," Mayam said. "I'm not stupid enough to take out life support. This wasn't some random impulse action."

Sue crossed her arms, doing her best to put on Dan's confidence in a situation that terrified her to her bones. With someone who didn't know the ship's systems well enough to safely modify the systems updates, it might as well have been an impulse action

Even Sue herself didn't know the software well enough to make those kinds of changes.

"You haven't seen the screens I do in the command center," Sue said. "You have no idea what you've changed, what effects every single change has. Humanity has never built anything as complex as *Bellagos* and ships like her. The changes cascade. The changes are *still* cascading, and even I don't know what's going to fail next."

Mayam scowled, but her defiant stance softened.

"All I did was spike the update. Left instructions for how the changes would be carried out that overwrote the ones from Earth HQ. I modified our sensors and the sweep field in these passages. Nothing more than that. Getting your attention was the point. It worked."

Sue steeled herself for the lie, needing to know what kind of systems and coding knowledge she was up against.

"Then what was the point of rigging the sensors ship-wide to trigger alarms for no reason? When Evans and I took Liam out to calm him down, Liam who is *still* a frightened little boy who needs his father, we couldn't help but notice the trouble they're having in the frozen food pod. Every single bowl sets off the alarm, even when you're nowhere near their boundary."

"I never touched those systems!" Mayam finally took a step back. "The only thing that changed is in here, in the maintenance passages."

Dan followed the step backward with a near-charge forward of his own. His voice was colder than the depths of the frozen food pod, and all the more dangerous for it.

"Chief Warrell has asked you repeatedly about the health and whereabouts of several of her crew members. Liam McHugh, his father, and Senior Tech Evans, to be specific. If you have any expectations of continuing this mission outside of a prison pod, which I will *happily* create just for you, answer her. Now."

"I'm already in prison," Mayam said, her whole body seeming to deflate. "We all are. Some of us just can't manage to pretend it's anything else. Liam and his father are fine. So is everyone else. They're in a storage pod not far from here. Did you really believe I would hurt them, Uncle Dan? Hurt a little boy?"

"You did hurt Liam," Dan said in a softer voice. "You took his father away. The boy had no idea where, or why. How many other people have you hurt and upset, Mayam? What did you think you could possibly gain with all this?"

Mayam stared into Dan's eyes, leaving Sue free to watch the three who were with her. The woman and two men were still and silent, either looking at Mayam or at the gray floor. They might have been willing to follow her, to respond to her actions or whatever she accomplished. But without her, they should be easy to calm down.

And easy to control. Direct where Sue wanted them to go.

"We don't have any prison pods onboard," Sue said, looking at the other three. "But we have plans to convert pods if the need ever arises. I don't want to do that, not now, not ever if I can help it. We need every crewmember to help make this mission a success."

She shifted her gaze to Mayam. "What you're doing is causing the kind of disruption we most need to avoid. More and more people are getting upset, and not just the families of people you abducted. I'm sure you have no idea what's happening since you're been hidden away out here. We *are* losing vital systems. Not just sensors, either. Food production is faltering. People know there's trouble. We're one of the first few colonization ships to ever leave Earth, but we know what happens in big communities or sailing ships. When people lose confidence, everything starts to break down."

Dan picked up on her lead exactly like Sue hoped.

"You know that's what I spent decades dealing with back on Earth," he said. "I watched systems break down, in uglier ways than you can imagine. Ways I don't ever want you or anyone else on board to experience. If we end up with riots on a contained ship because of this kind of disruption, exactly how do you think Chief Warrell should handle that?"

Chapter 12

Mayam stood with her arms crossed staring up at Dan, leaving Sue wondering if she'd mimicked the gesture in her uncle when she was growing up. The three behind Mayam shifted their feet and glanced nervously at each other.

Martinez spoke up from beside Sue.

"We don't have the capacity or crew to handle anything like this in Maintenance, much less riots or a bunch of people locked up. Just me being offline right now is going to play hell with our schedules. Especially in the emergency situation you created. You get too many of us trapped back here or trying to deal with the trouble the corrupted update has caused, and life support systems won't have to fail."

He paused, looking at Mayam and the other three for a few seconds. "If this keeps up, *Bellagos* will take herself apart all around us. But at least your *inconvenience* would be at an end, right?"

Slowly enough that it would have been easy to miss if Sue hadn't been watching for it, the three behind Mayam moved back a step. They moved closer together, too, almost shoulder to shoulder, leaving Mayam standing alone.

"I'm not stupid," Mayam said so quietly that Sue had to strain to hear her. "I'm not a kid, either. I don't want everyone to die." She shook her head. "I don't want *anyone* to die. I just don't want this. I never did. No one should have been hauled out here against their will."

Dan nodded, and the warmth and sympathy in his face stirred up a pleasant heat in Sue's middle, even while her eyes prickled with tears.

"You were brought against your will, you're right. That wasn't fair." He looked at all of the group behind Mayam. "It wasn't fair to any of you. I can't change it, but I can say I'm sorry. I truly am. I can't speak for all of your families, but I know my brother was thrilled to be able to give you this chance to help build a new human homeworld. That was your mother's dream, too."

Mayam turned her head to the side, but not before Sue saw her blinking back tears.

"I know. I remember her talking about it before she died. Barely, but I remember. This all might have been different if she were here. Or I might hate it even more with both of them telling me how wonderful it is. How damn *lucky* I am to be here."

Jacinda spoke then, surprising Sue until she realized Mayam was only a couple of years younger.

"Having them both here might have helped a little. Both my mothers are, and my bio-dad. They drove me crazy the whole time I lived with them, though, carrying on about The Great Dream and Carrying Humanity to the Stars and all the other capitalized slogans they came up with."

Mayam looked Jacinda up and down, her eyes narrowed.

"You believe in all that stuff?" she said. "All the hype and propaganda?"

Jacinda shrugged, holding up one hand.

"Not exactly the way my moms put it, no. I'm pretty sure

the galaxy would have been just fine without a bunch of humans cluttering up the place like we did on Earth. Probably better off. I didn't much like feeling like I had no choice in being here myself. But I'd rather see it work than see it all fall apart around us."

"I was angry when I asked you before," Sue said, "so let me try again. What would make this better? We all know what we *can't* do to change things. What are your ideas for what we *can* do?"

Mayam turned her head, then her whole body to face the three behind her. A few steps behind her now, and all of them staring at their feet. The other young woman finally raised her head.

Sue saw her give a sad half-smile, then shake her head. Leaving Mayam on her own, exactly as Sue expected.

A soft sigh from Dan let her know he'd expected the same.

Mayam turned slowly, blinking back tears again and rolling her eyes at the same time.

"Okay, now that I know where we all stand," she said. "We want...*I* want to have a say in what happens here. What I'm supposed to do. What's supposed to happen for the rest of this journey I won't live to see the end of."

"You have as much right to choose what you do as the rest of us," Dan said, not quite back to his military voice, but edging toward it.

Mayam shook her head, hands on her slender hips again.

"No, Uncle Dan, we don't. We all got the same training from the second we stepped on board. Or the second we were carried on board, too many of us. We serve the same apprenticeships, get sorted into the career paths *you* or Earth HQ say will suit us best. I'm supposed to get funneled into Security like a good little drone. Preparing us to live useful lives to best serve the mission. Not one thought given to what would serve ourselves or make us happy."

"That's what we're all doing," Dan said, holding up both hands. "But maybe things can change. You're right. Odds are high you won't live to see the end of this mission, but some of you might. I know I won't. So what you want and how you want to run things matters."

"The rules we have aren't inflexible," Sue said. The three behind Mayam shifted, paying attention now. "Earth HQ only gave us guidelines. No one knew for sure how any of this would go, and they can't exactly punish us. I'll admit I wondered if that's what they were doing with that damn botched systems update. Trying to shake us up so we'll keep paying attention to them instead of depending more and more on ourselves."

"I know what all this trouble has really caused," Jacinda said. "Everyone on the Security side does. People on board got a reminder that we're all in trapped together in a huge metal ship in the dead of space. Even if they'd made their peace with our situation, worked out how to live with it, you pushed it into their faces. If you wanted everyone to be more aware of that, you succeeded."

Jacinda and Mayam locked gazes, and Sue had no doubt the two of them understood each other in a way neither she or Dan ever would.

After all, she and Dan and others of their generation had not only chosen to come on this mission, they'd fought for the chance.

Mayam blew air out through her lips.

"That wasn't quite what we were trying to do, but maybe it's a good thing. I never forget that for a second. I wanted to start with letting us choose what we want to study once we get past the basics. What we want to learn how to do. Maybe learn as many different duties as we can. I know we must have all the functions on *Bellagos* filled, and we'll have to deal with that. But maybe if we branch out and learn more, we could rotate through."

Dan smiled at Sue, surprising her yet again when he winked.

"I'm on my third career, hoping to have more ahead. And, I've been resisting Earth HQ's idea of how I could best support the mission since before I came onboard. I'm not the one in charge, but I can't think of any reason to argue. What do you think, Chief?"

"I'm not in charge either," Sue said. "Humans couldn't possibly go out into space without recreating committees and other such nonsense, no matter what they call it. I suspect it would do crewmembers a hell of a lot of good to know more about how *Bellagos* operates. How fragile she is, and how strong. What you ask makes sense to me."

Sue stepped forward and held out her hand to Mayam.

"I'll bring it up, I promise. As soon as everyone is back with their families. And, if you agree to come to the command pod so you can see how many systems you actually disrupted whether you meant to or not."

Before Mayam could respond, a low thud rumbled through the floor, and all the harsh overhead lights in the passages they could see switched on at full strength. Screeching alarms from all seven comms had everyone scrambling to silence them.

"…please, Chief. Report and confirm status."

Sue raised her comm, unable to hold back a wide grin. For the first time in her life, she welcomed the stim-itch flaring up over her whole body with the jolt of adrenaline.

"Here and fine, Tima. Get word back from Earth HQ? A new update?"

"Glad to hear your voice, ma'am. We got word from HQ, but no new update. After I verified the missing or

Invalid crewmembers, I dug into the systems interface and located code that didn't fit protocol. Earth HQ said to act on our own best information while they analyze the problem. So I removed that code and rolled back to the last clean version. When you give the word, HQ will resend the update, hardened against that code. Crew numbers are back to full, all on the tracking board."

"I think you and Mayam here will have a lot to talk about," Sue said, laughing. "You both seem to know the software better than I do. Maybe it's past time I stopped being so hands-off with the software that keeps this place running myself. Well done not *quite* obeying orders, Tima. I knew I could train that rule-following out of you. You ready to stay on shift for a few more hours?"

Sue could just about see her second, mouth opening and closing, cheeks red, blinking. Trying to decide whether she'd done good or bad.

Tima's calm, confident voice shifted the balance toward good.

"Thank you, ma'am. Ready and glad to stand for a full shift."

"I'll bring everyone out and check in," Sue said. "Then I'm off for at least a full sleep cycle. Three if I can manage it. Call in someone else when you need a break, hold steady on the old systems software. The rest will be there when we're all ready to face it."

Chapter 13

THE CLASSROOM POD had been designed for older students —well into their second decade and even beginning their third—but Sue was surprised to feel a bit cramped.

The space was the full dimensions of a standard living pod without any walls or divisions, so that didn't quite make sense. Four rows of long white tables left plenty of room for everyone, even with a larger crowd than anyone expected for the last day of their first software coding workshop.

Every attendee had an arm's length on both sides. The white chairs weren't nearly as comfortable as Sue's in her command pod, but they were workable. The lighting was set to full Earth daylight and reflected nicely off the bright yellow walls. Even the full-wall instructional monitor up front showed an open vista of a calm Earth ocean around the unused edges, adding to the expansive feeling.

A fresh ocean breeze completed the scene and somehow enhanced concentration rather than distracting it.

Sue finally decided the confines around her physical body weren't causing her discomfort. She simply wasn't used to being in a room full of thirty people. They ranged from members of her own Systems and Security Team to Martinez from Maintenance to at least one from every occupation onboard *Bellagos*.

The ages ranged as well, and Sue and Dan were far from the only gray heads in attendance.

Up front, Dan's niece Mayam and Sue's second-in-command Tima continued to do a fine job of explaining the basics of the code language that made everything surrounding them function. Mayam in particular had high color and obvious enthusiasm that warmed Sue's heart.

Whether Mayam decided to stay in teaching or working in code or transitioned into her original path of Security, she'd be a natural at the job.

Sue felt a bit less happy about Tima taking so well to teaching, but couldn't deny she was good at it.

Dan's chair did sit quite a bit closer than was required, and Sue was happier about that by the day. Since she and everyone else in Systems and Security had gone back to regular leisure days, more than a few of hers had coordinated with Dan's.

It seemed wanting the company of another human outside of work hours wasn't quite as far behind Sue as she'd thought.

Not when it was the right human.

He caught her glancing his way and winked with the half-smile that spoke volumes. Sue knew her cheeks and throat were flushed from memory and promise, but she didn't care. She focused on the front of the classroom just as Mayam switched the display to full ocean.

"Everyone has done a fantastic job this week," she said, beaming at Tima, then at Sue. "We appreciate the opportunity more than we can say, and we hope you all enjoyed it as much as we did."

Both of them basked in well-deserved, hearty applause.

Sue felt like her brain was straining at the edges, and she'd taken more notes than when she was a student herself decades ago.

And she was thrilled to admit that understanding how the software was constructed was already helping her manage onboard systems.

The replacement update from Earth HQ had installed flawlessly, and Sue expected the same from future versions. No one would be touching live software anytime soon, or making changes to existing systems.

But she had no doubt teaching the next generation of programmers would be vital to their mission's independence, and their eventual success.

The changes they were making in this room—and in similar classrooms all over *Bellagos*—would cascade and grow and branch off into the future in unpredictable ways.

Exactly as Mayam's changes to ship systems had not so long ago.

But Sue was certain the simple fact of crewmembers working together now, with full understanding and growing respect for the vital role they all filled, would help make these new changes positive ones.

And leave everyone onboard *Bellagos* and future generations stretching all the way forward to their eventual settlement on Junos 7 better equipped to handle whatever came their way.

Dan stood and walked to the front of the room and Sue joined him, her cheeks flaming again when he reached for her hand. She held tight and spoke over the general commotion of people getting ready to leave.

"We want to thank both Mayam and Tima for doing such a great job teaching," she said. "As well as congratulate ourselves and everyone else on a job well done keeping up with them."

"Everyone in this room has earned a treat," Dan said.

At a tap on Sue's comm, the doors to the side opened. Liam McHugh pushed a hover-cart full of double-sided frozen treat bowls, head high and bursting with pride. Liam's father followed close behind with Senior Tech Evans, both pushing silver hover-carts Sue knew were full of almost every flavor people could put into those bowls.

Cassie from the frozen treat pod came last. Her smile was a thousand light years from the fake customer service version Sue had seen when none of them had any idea what they were facing.

More importantly, Sue knew the hover-cart Cassie pushed was full of chocolate, cherry, and her own favorite mix of the two.

As everyone else gathered around the celebratory treats, Sue leaned up and whispered in Dan's ear, breathing in the warm scent of his skin.

"We still on for a private celebration later, Mr. Greenwell?"

This time she got his full smile, and went a bit weak in the knees.

"You bet we are, Chief. *Bellagos* will just have to manage without us for a couple of leisure days."

Sue surprised herself by kissing Dan full on the mouth, right there in view of the whole group.

"Good."

ABOUT KARI

A science fiction fan from the first time she caught a grainy black and white rerun of *Lost in Space*, Kari Kilgore's wanderlust and imagination lead her all over the world on grand adventures. Her heart and family bring her home to her native Appalachian Mountains of Virginia. From that solid base, she and her husband Jason A. Adams bring those adventures to life in fiction.

Kari writes science fiction, fantasy, romance, and contemporary fiction, and she's happiest when she surprises herself. She lives at the end of a long dirt road in the middle of the woods with Jason, various house critters, and wildlife they're better off not knowing more about.

The Confidential Adventure Club

For Kari's exclusive free After The End stories and deleted scenes, discounts, early pre-sale releases, adorable pet photos, and a whole lot more not available anywhere else, visit The Confidential Adventure Club at www.smarturl.it/c-a-club.

Hope to see you there!

www.karikilgore.com
www.spiralpublishing.net

ALSO BY KARI KILGORE

I hope you enjoyed *The Changes Cascade* as much as I enjoyed writing it. For more space opera and galactic empire stories, be sure to keep an eye out for Dispatches from the Galaxy at www.dispatchesfromthegalaxy.com.

For more science fiction from both me and Jason A. Adams, visit Spiral Publishing's Science Fiction page at www.spiralpublishing.net/book-tag/science-fiction.

Be the first to know about release dates and check out more of my fiction across almost every genre at www.karikilgore.com.

The Confidential Adventure Club

Want more fiction from Kari, including stories, discounts, and box sets not available anywhere else? Want to hear about locations, research, and other cool things that inspired this story and beyond? Want all that and adorable pet photos, too?

Join The Confidential Adventure Club and get a thank you gift of a free short story and a whole lot more at www.smarturl.it/c-a-club.

Hope to see you there!

Dispatches from the Galaxy Stories:

Restricted Species

The Becalmed

The Garbage Belt

Plurapod Pathogen

The Storms of Future Past Series:

Dreaming the Storm

Joining the Storm

Into the Storm

Fighting the Storm

Sensing the Storm: A Storms of Future Past Prequel Story

Storms of the Heart: A Storms of Future Past Romance

Storms of Future Past Books One through Four Collection

The Voices through Time Series:

Songs in the Mountain

Secrets in the Land

Walking the Ghosts: A Voices through Time Novella

Terminalia Short Stories:

Terminalia

Little Five

Novels:

Until Death

The Dream Thief

Hand Me Downs

Novellas:

Legacy of the Land

In the Pines

DNA Never Lies

Collections:

Fantastic Women: A Dark Fantasy Novella Trio

Fantastic Shorts: Volume 1

Near Future Forward (with Jason A. Adams)

Fantastic Shorts: Volume 2

Partners in Romance (with Jason A. Adams)

Short Stories:

Renovations, Intentions, The Seeds of Love, Wicked Bone, The Sound of Murder, Reflections, The Last Dragonkeeper, The Earworms, Odds and Endings, Dawn Visitor, The Spider Who Ate the Elephant, The Worry Trap, An Adventure Well Begun, Morning Glory, The Heart Is the Strongest, The Sweetest Trouble, Happily Ever After in KrampusLand, The Real Treasure in Cairo, Soul Deep

www.ingramcontent.com/pod-product-compliance
Lightning Source LLC
Chambersburg PA
CBHW032042180726
48284CB00008B/2716